D0572898

JELLYBEAN
MOUSE

Story by Philip Roy

Art by Andrea Torrey Balsara

RONSDALE PRESS

"John?"

"Mmmhmm?"

"I'm bored."

"Mmmhmm?"

"I'm bored, John.
Can we do something
exciting today?"

"Actually, Happy, today we have to go to the laundromat."

"Is that where you wash clothes?"

"Yes."

"Let's not do that today, John. Let's do something else."

"But our clothes are dirty, Happy."

"No, they're not.
They're just right."

"Happy, they're pretty stinky. We have to wash our clothes sometimes or we won't feel good about ourselves."

"John, I always feel good about myself and I never wash my pocket."

"That's the place that needs washing the most."

"You can't wash my pocket! It won't feel like home anymore. You want me to feel at home, don't you?"

"Happy, I bet you will really like it after we wash it."

"No, I won't. I will hate it. The laundromat is the most boring place in the whole world. I want to do something exciting, like . . . work on a sailing ship."

"A sailing ship?"

"Yes. A navy ship."

"A navy ship? But . . . what if it goes to war?"

"*Especially* if it goes to war."

"But . . . what if it gets hit by a cannonball and starts to sink?"

"That's the most exciting part!"

"But . . . what if it sinks, and it's just you on the water?"

"Actually, I meant a pirate ship."

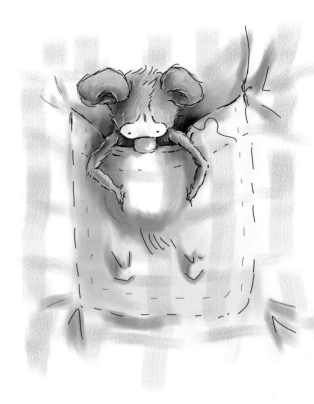

"A pirate ship?"

"Yes. Because pirates never wash their clothes."

(later)

"John! Look! There's a bowling alley. Let's go bowling."

"Maybe after we wash our clothes."

"No. I won't feel like it then. Look! There's the skating rink. Let's go skating."

Myrtle's
Fine Foods

SOAPY SUD
LAUNDRY

"Maybe after."

"Hmmmf! It's always *after*.
Oh! The grocery store!
We'd better buy groceries, John.
We might get hungry."

"I don't think so, Happy.
The laundromat is really
warm. Our groceries
might go bad."

Candy $1/lb.
Bananas .99¢/lb
Cheeses $1.99/lb

Specials
"It's always fun at
Myrtle's!"

"Hmmmf! Is this the laundromat?"

"Yes."

"Hmmmf! Boring! John?"

"What?"

"What's that?"

"That? That's a jellybean machine."

"A *jellybean machine?*"

"Yes. You have to . . . Happy? Happy?"

"John! I need your help!
The jellybean machine
won't give me any jellybeans.
I think it's broken."

"You have to put a
quarter in it."

"Ohhh, can I have a
quarter, please?"

"Sorry, Happy. I have only enough quarters to wash our clothes."

"You don't need money to wash clothes, John. You only need soap."

"The machines need quarters, Happy."

"They take money, too?"

"Yes."

"Hmmm! Oh, well . . . then just give me *one* quarter."

"Sorry, Happy, I need them all."

"You need them *all* . . . for *yourself*?"

"For the *wash*. You know what, Happy? Sometimes people drop coins under the machines. I bet if you looked, you might find a quarter."

"Hmmm. That's like treasure hunting, isn't it?"

"Sort of."

"Okay. I'll be right back...."

"Look, John! I found one!"

"That's a nickel."

"It is?"

"Yes."

"Hmmmf! Just wait, John. I'll be right back..."

"...*pant, pant* ...I found one, John...*pant, pant*...
Treasure hunting sure is hard work."

"Yes. This is a quarter."

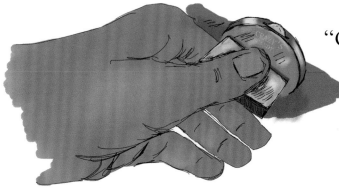

"Quick! Let's put it in the machine, John, and get our jellybeans."

"Okay. Here we go."

"Hmmm. How long is it supposed to take?"

"It didn't work."

"*What*? It didn't work?"

"Sometimes these machines don't work."

"*They take our money, and they don't work?*"

"Sometimes."

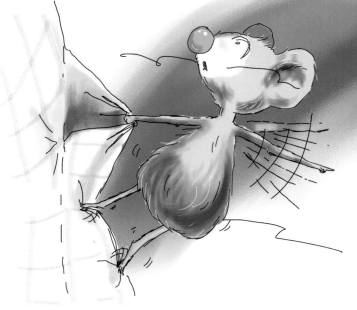

"Quick, John! Hit the machine!"

"What?"

"When no one's looking. Just hit it a little."

"Happy, I don't think I should."

"Yes, you should, John. It took our money!"

"Well, maybe just a tap...There."

"Harder, John."

"I don't know, Happy. I don't want to break it."

"You won't break it, John. These machines are really strong."

"Well, maybe a little bit harder...There."

"Bang it, John!"

"Ummmf!!! Oh! Wow!"

"OH . . . MY . . . STARS!

Look at all the lovely jellybeans!"

"Gee, Happy, I don't think we were supposed to get so many."

"Yes, we were, John. That's what a jellybean machine does. Isn't a laundromat a great place, John?"

"I guess so."

"Mmmmmmmmm . . . these are the best jellybeans ever. Let's sit on the bench and watch our clothes go around and eat our jellybeans. Okay, John?"

"Okay."

"You know what, John?"

"What?"

"I love laundromats."

"That's nice, Happy. Do you still want to go bowling?"

"Hmmm . . . do they have a jellybean machine there?"

"I don't know."

"Well . . . maybe not today."

(bedtime)

"John?"

"Mmmhmm?"

"It was a pretty exciting day today. Do you think we could go to the laundromat tomorrow?"

"I don't think so, Happy.
Our clothes are clean."

"My pocket's dirty."

"Your pocket's dirty *already*?
How could it get dirty so fast?"

"I don't know. It just is."

"Well, if it's just your pocket, I think
we can clean that at home. We don't need
to go all the way to the laundromat."

"Hmmmf! Just a minute, John,
I'll be right back..."

"John?"

"What?"

"I think we better go to the laundromat tomorrow. I spilled milk on your pants and they're getting pretty stinky. We don't want to go around in stinky clothes. It doesn't feel good."

"Hmmmmm . . .
Okay, Happy, we'll see.
Good night."

"Good night, John."

"John?"

"What?"

"Have you ever crawled under a washing machine before?"

"No."

"It's pretty exciting. Okay, good night, John."

"Good night, Happy."

The End

For every child who has ever thought of a mouse as a friend – P.R.

To "Mehrkatie" & "Kaymehra": two of the very best – A.T.B.

PHILIP ROY divides his time between Ontario and Nova Scotia
with his wife Leila, their kids and their cat. Visit Philip at www.philiproy.ca.

ANDREA TORREY BALSARA lives with her family and motley retinue of
critters in Bowmanville, Ontario. Visit Andrea at www.torreybalsara.com.

JELLYBEAN MOUSE
Text Copyright © 2014 Philip Roy / Illustrations Copyright © 2014 Andrea Torrey Balsara

RONSDALE PRESS
3350 West 21st Avenue, Vancouver, B.C., Canada, V6S 1G7
www.ronsdalepress.com

Ronsdale Press wishes to thank the following for their support of its publishing program:
the Canada Council for the Arts, the Government of Canada through the Canada Book Fund,
the British Columbia Arts Council, and the Province of British Columbia through
the British Columbia Book Publishing Tax Credit program.

Library and Archives Canada Cataloguing in Publication

Roy, Philip, 1960–, author
Jellybean mouse / Philip Roy; Andrea Torrey Balsara, illustrator.

(Happy the pocket mouse; book II)
ISBN 978-1-55380-344-7 (bound)

I. Balsara, Andrea Torrey, illustrator II. Title.

PS8635.O91144J45 2014   jC813'.6   C2014-905619-2

Printed in Canada on FSC paper by Friesens, Manitoba